Just Like Sisters

LouAnn Gaeddert

Just Like Sisters

illustrated by Gail Owens

Weekly Reader Books
Middletown, Connecticut

Weekly Reader Books Edition published
by arrangement with E.P. Dutton

2 3 4 5 / 86 85 84 83

for *my* sister, Priscilla Meldrim

1

Carrie Clark sat on the floor and began to empty the bottom drawer in her dresser.

"Out," she shouted aloud as she stuffed an old spelling notebook into a plastic garbage bag.

"Out," she shouted again as a traffic-light picture she had painted in kindergarten followed the notebook.

Out. Out. Out. The drawer was finally empty and the garbage bag was full.

"Congratulations, Carrie." Mother had turned off the vacuum cleaner in the hall and stood in the doorway.

Carrie held up a nursery-school picture and they both laughed. It showed three people and a black cat. The cat was almost as big as the father. You could tell it was Carrie's father because he wore glasses. MY FAMILY was written in large, uneven letters under the people. A round yellow sun shone over them.

Carrie opened the next drawer and pulled out a

bathing suit. They both laughed as she held it against herself. It hardly covered her navel, let alone the important parts of her body.

"I wonder why we saved that," Mother said as she put the bathing suit on one of the beds. "We'll take everything that is too small to the clothing box at church."

Carrie couldn't believe what she was hearing. She knew why they had saved it. All the outgrown clothes had been saved for the little sister who had never been born. Only last year Mother had cried as she gave away the carriage and all the baby clothes.

"We're very happy with the one child we have," she had said as she hugged Carrie so tightly that it hurt. "And Daddy and I have decided to forget about other children. Obviously there just aren't going to be any."

"But I don't want to be an only child," Carrie had wailed. Then she had felt sorry. Her parents had wanted a baby as much as she had wanted one. So she had smiled at Mother, and they had never talked about the hoped-for little sister again.

And this summer Carrie would not be an only child. This summer she was going to have a sister— almost a twin sister. Kate was really her cousin, just three months older than Carrie and in the same grade. Not enough older to be bossy like her friend Alice's sister. Carrie and Kate Clark, she said to herself. *The Clark girls*. She liked those words.

"It's good to get all these things cleaned out," Mother said as she added three sweaters to the pile of

clothes on the bed. "Kate will sleep here tonight because Uncle Richard will be sleeping in my sewing room. After he leaves, she may want to move in there."

"Why would she want to do that? She'll want to sleep here. I know she will. She's an only child, too. She's been sleeping alone all her life."

"She may want privacy. You may both want to get away from one another before the summer is over."

"Never," said Carrie. "I just wish we'd known she was coming before last night, so I could have made more plans. Did you call Uncle Richard back and tell him to bring Kate's bike?"

"Yes," said Mother.

"Do you think she likes to play Monopoly?"

"Probably," said Mother.

"Do you think she'll like Ebony?" Carrie asked as a big black cat strolled into the room and climbed into her lap.

"I hope so."

"I just wish we'd known earlier."

Mother sat down beside Carrie. "I know you like to plan, but there are some things we just can't plan. I guess you should know that Kate's parents are having problems. That's why Uncle Richard is bringing her here for the summer."

"What kinds of problems?"

"I don't know. He just said problems. That's enough for us to know. We will not ask Kate about them. Don't forget that. We will not ask Kate."

"We'll have such a good time, she'll forget all about problems," Carrie said firmly. "What are we going to have for dinner?"

"Spaghetti."

"Good choice. All kids like spaghetti."

"I'm glad you approve." Mother kissed the top of Carrie's head.

By five o'clock the aroma of the sauce was wafting up to Carrie's room. The room was spotless, and three drawers of her dresser and half of her closet were empty, just waiting for Kate's things. Carrie's hair was washed but still wet. She pulled a comb through her short, dark curls. She hadn't seen Kate for several years, but she would never forget her beautiful hair, long and golden. She'd been inches taller than Carrie then. Was she still taller? Carrie had grown a lot. But Kate had probably grown, too.

She put on her new green shorts with a matching T-shirt and strapped sandals on her feet. She went downstairs to set the table, and then she sat down on the swing on the porch to plan.

Tomorrow they'd go to church. Then they'd probably have a big dinner. Then Uncle Richard would leave. Then maybe they could go to the lake for a swim. Then maybe Daddy would take them out for hamburgers—he often did on Sunday nights. They'd talk late into the night.

"Hey, Mother," Carrie shouted. "Do you think Kate knows how to swim?"

"I don't know."

"Do you think she likes croquet?"

"I don't know."

"I hope she likes to weed," said Daddy as he came up on the porch, all sweaty from mowing the lawn. He took off his glasses and mopped his face with the sleeve of his shirt.

"Nobody likes to weed," said Carrie. "You aren't going to ask her to weed, are you? She's our guest."

"She will be a member of our family for the summer," said Daddy as Mother came and kissed him on the cheek.

"You're going to make her work?"

"We'll expect her to do about what you do."

"But I thought that since I would have company, I wouldn't . . ."

"You thought you'd be excused from your chores?" Mother laughed. "Sorry, old dear, but there will still be a dishwasher to load and furniture to dust. . . ."

"And weeds in the garden," added Daddy.

"But I hadn't planned on working."

" 'The best-laid schemes o' mice an' men gang aft a-gley.' " Daddy liked to quote Robert Burns, who wrote poems in Old Scots, a language that sounded like English—but not quite.

He and Mother went inside.

Carrie made plans for Monday—swimming lessons and then a picnic at the lake. Tuesday—swimming lessons and then maybe Alice could come for lunch. She hoped Kate and Alice would like one another.

6

Wednesday they might have a croquet tournament with Paul and Danny Lang, who lived next door. They didn't think about anything except baseball, but they were useful for games. If it rained, they might come over and play Monopoly.

Sometime they would have to work in a trip to the library, although Carrie couldn't see when there would be time to read. That's what she'd done previous summers—before she'd had a sister.

Maybe she should make a list of all the things there were to do. Then she could give the list to Kate and let Kate choose on certain days. That would be nice. She went to the den, sat down at the desk, and wrote all the games she had and all of the activities she could think of. It ran to three sheets of paper. She was surprised when she had finished to hear the clock strike seven.

"Where are they?" she asked as she went back to the porch.

She sat down next to Daddy, who smelled all soapy after his shower. Daddy and Mother were sipping drinks. Mother handed Carrie a can of soda.

"They'll be here," she said.

"But they're late."

"It takes at least four hours to drive from their part of New Jersey to our part of New York. Maybe they got a late start or took a wrong turn. In the meantime, it's nice to just sit." Mother taught English in the high school. She always thought it was nice to just sit for about two weeks after school ended.

7

A car was coming slowly down the road. Carrie jumped up and ran out on the lawn.

"Hi, Mrs. Clark," a boy shouted and then speeded up and went on.

"A student from my senior honors class two years ago," Mother explained.

Carrie sat down on the steps and Ebony crawled into her lap. Mother and Daddy discussed a problem at the plant. Problems at the plant were always dull, so Carrie tried to think of more things that she and Kate could do.

2

It was almost dark and Carrie's stomach was growling from hunger. As if she could hear it, Mother suggested that they go ahead and eat. She went into the house. Carrie was about to follow when out of nowhere—she hadn't heard the motor—a car pulled into the driveway.

Daddy strode across the porch and the lawn, arriving at the car just as Uncle Richard got out. They slapped one another on the back and shouted greetings. "Good to see you." "Sorry we're late." Carrie wondered why they didn't kiss. They were brothers after all. Well, she would kiss her new sister. She ran forward. The light was on inside the car and Carrie could see Kate sitting there, staring straight ahead.

"Hi, Kate," Carrie called as she reached for the door handle. It didn't move. "Hey, unlock the door."

Kate reached over and opened the door, but she did not get out. Why? Was she sick? She didn't look sick.

"Come on, Kate," Carrie begged. "I've made lots of

9

space for you in my room. Bring your things in. We're going to have a great time this summer. Did you bring your bike? Do you like . . ." Carrie stopped. Her cousin was not even looking at her.

"Come get your bike," Uncle Richard called. Carrie went to the back of the car. Uncle Richard set the bike—a black ten-speed racer—on the driveway and leaned over and kissed Carrie.

"You're still a cute little mosquito," he said as he ruffled her curls.

Mosquito indeed. She'd grown three inches in the last year alone. But when Kate finally got out of the car, Carrie could see why Uncle Richard thought she was small. Kate was so tall. Her hair was as beautiful as ever. Carrie decided to start all over again with Kate.

"Hi," she said, as if she had not said that already. "Your hair is just as pretty as I remembered it."

Kate didn't say anything.

"We'll put your racer beside my old clunker." Carrie rolled the bike into the garage and then went back to the car to help Kate carry in her things.

Mother was waiting for them at the door. "Hello, Kate. We're so glad you've come." Her voice was melty and she reached out to hug Kate. Kate turned away, so that Mother could only give her a quick peck in the air near her cheek. "Dinner will be ready in a few minutes," she said. "You can take your things directly upstairs."

Carrie lugged the large suitcase, anxious to show Kate that she was strong even though she was small. Kate carried two shopping bags.

"Which bed would you like?" Carrie asked as they entered the room.

"I don't care." Those were the first words Kate had spoken since she arrived.

"They are just the same and they both have clean sheets, so I'll sleep in the one next to the wall. I usually sleep there. You can sleep in this one."

Kate sat on the bed. She didn't look around at Carrie's nice clean room. She just sat. Carrie opened the empty drawers.

"These are for your things." She opened the closet door. "And here is more space for you."

"Thanks," said Kate without looking up.

"I'm really glad you've come. I've planned all kinds of fun things we can do together this summer. We'll be just like sisters."

"Sisters fight," said Kate.

Kate didn't speak during dinner and Uncle Richard said very little. Daddy did the talking. He boomed on and on about his tomato plants, and the blight on his roses, and the size of the squashes he'd grown last year. Mother put in a few words and Carrie, too, tried to help out with conversation. None of them sounded like themselves. Their voices were too loud and they laughed when nothing was funny.

The spaghetti was delicious. That was the only

good thing to be said about the meal. Mother and Carrie cleared away the plates, and then Mother came back to the table with coffee.

"We have lime sherbet and chocolate ice cream," she announced. "Which would you like, Kate?"

"I don't care," said Kate.

Mother started to say something, then stopped. "I guess we'll all have sherbet. It will be refreshing after the spaghetti."

"Mighty good spaghetti," boomed Daddy.

"Sure was," added Carrie.

Uncle Richard and Kate said nothing.

Carrie ate her sherbet and then jumped up and began clearing the table. Kate did not help her. Carrie loaded the dishwasher. She cleaned the sink, a job she loathed. She swept the floor. Anything was easier than trying to talk with people who just sat in silence, looking at you. At last, when she could think of nothing else to do in the kitchen, she went back to the dining room, yawning.

"I think I'll go to bed and read," she said.

"What a good idea." Mother sounded as if Carrie had just said something clever. "Why don't you go up with her, Kate?"

Kate didn't say anything, but she got up and followed Carrie.

"I have lots of books," Carrie said, pointing to her bookcase. "What kinds do you like?"

"I only read horse books and sports books," said Kate. "And I've brought my own." Kate took a book out of one of her shopping bags and put it on the bed. That was the last thing she said that night.

Kate did not go to church with Carrie and her parents. She and Uncle Richard had things to talk about, Mother explained. They all had dinner in the early afternoon. When Uncle Richard got ready to leave, Kate walked with him to his car. Carrie and her parents stayed on the porch, watching and then waving. Kate stood in the driveway for a long time. Then she walked around to the back of the house. Carrie started to follow, but her father held her back.

"We'll give Kate a little time and then we'll all go to the lake," he said.

"And then we'll go out for hamburgers?" she asked.

"Yes." He hugged Carrie.

"What's the matter with Kate anyway? She won't even talk with me."

Daddy looked at Mother and they both looked at Carrie.

"Kate has been very unhappy," he explained slowly. "Aunt Janet has moved to New York City. . . ."

"Without Kate?"

"Without Kate. She and Uncle Richard still live in New Jersey."

"Who takes care of them?"

"They take care of themselves. Uncle Richard brought Kate to stay here for the summer because he thought she would be happier with us, and he didn't

14

want her to be alone all day while he is at work. We'll give Kate time to think and to feel. We'll try to be patient and understanding and hope that she will be happy with us."

"What about Aunt Janet?" Carrie asked, putting her arms around her own mother.

"She has a small apartment and a good job designing fabrics," said Mother.

"Has Kate been to visit her?"

"No," said Mother.

"Why not?"

"I don't know. We've told you everything Uncle Richard has told us, so please don't ask any more questions. And don't ask Kate questions either." Mother sighed.

Daddy straighted his shoulders and walked across the porch to where he could look into the backyard. "Come on, Kate," he called. "Get your bathing suit on. We're going to the lake for a swim, and then out for hamburgers."

Kate went but she did not swim. Instead she took the towel Mother gave her and went and sat on a rock beyond the sandy area. There she sat, staring out across the water, while Mother talked to one of her friends on the beach and Carrie and her father swam out to the raft. It was the kind of hot, heavy day when the water felt most delicious. Carrie stayed in the water even after her father had gone in to dry in the sun.

"Perhaps you'll want to learn to swim this summer," Mother said to Kate as they walked toward the car. "Lessons start tomorrow and will be held every weekday morning for six weeks."

"I can swim."

"Good. Then you can take lessons with Carrie, and at the end of the summer you'll swim even better than you do now. And you will meet other young people." Mother reached out to hug Kate, who sidled away.

Carrie had a super hamburger and a coffee shake. As soon as she got home, she took a shower, put on her pajamas and went out on the porch to swing and cool off. Kate was already in bed with the sheet pulled up over her head when Carrie went upstairs again.

3

Nothing was better on Monday, and the weather was worse—hotter and stickier. In the future, Carrie and Kate would ride their bikes to the lake, but on the first day of swimming lessons Mother packed a lunch and drove them.

Carrie was not good at sports. She was never picked for any team until all of the good players had been chosen. She had taken the intermediate swimming class last year, but she had not passed all of the tests and so she would be taking it again this year.

In the car, Mother tried to find out which would be the right class for Kate. Yes, Kate had taken swimming lessons. There was a pool at her school. Yes, she was a good swimmer and she would be taking Junior Lifesaving in the fall.

"You might just as well start on Junior Lifesaving now," Mother said. "Although lake swimming is a little different from pool swimming."

"It sure is." Kate sounded disdainful. "You don't have a diving board. I like to dive."

Alice was already at the beach when they arrived and Carrie ran to her as to shelter in a storm. Skinny little Alice had never looked so beautiful. Best friends since kindergarten, Alice and Carrie never ran out of things to talk about.

"I'm going to be the oldest one in advanced beginners," Alice wailed while the two friends were still yards apart across the beach. Poor Alice. She was afraid of the water. Every year she came to swimming lessons determined to learn. Every year she tried; she just didn't make any progress.

"Come on, Kate," Carrie called back to her cousin. "I want you to meet my best friend." Carrie waited while Kate walked toward them slowly, kicking sand. "This is Alice. And this is my cousin Kate."

"Hi." Alice smiled so that her braces glinted in the sun. "I'm glad you're going to be here this summer."

"Another little shrimp," said Kate. She looked down at the two girls for a minute and then turned, stripped off her T-shirt and ran into the water.

"Big is not necessarily best," Carrie called after her.

Kate swam with strong strokes. When the instructor blew his whistle and motioned for her to come back to shore, she seemed not to hear. Instead she kept on swimming out to the raft, around it, and then back.

"I wish I could swim like that." Alice sighed.

The Junior Lifesaving class met first. There Kate did not look tall. There were only two other girls, both teenagers. One was Alice's bossy sister. There were also seven boys. One was Paul Lang. He was just about Kate's height, although he was a year older. When her lesson was over, Kate stayed out on the raft with some of the boys from her class.

Carrie's lesson was next. Then it was Alice's turn. Alice was the one who looked tall. Everyone else in the class was indeed younger.

At first Carrie hoped for some miracle that would make it possible for Alice to be promoted into the intermediate class. The miracle didn't happen. Alice stood in the water looking blue and miserable. When she tried to float, she stiffened and sank, coming up with a nose full of water. All that could be said for Alice's swimming was that she tried.

One of Alice's three brothers was in the beginners' class. It was depressing to watch him. He could swim almost as well as Alice, and he was only six years old. Alice's sister took him home when his lesson, the last of the day, was over.

Alice brought her sandwich to the Clarks' blanket, and Kate came in from the raft and sat on the very edge of the blanket with her back to the rest of them. Mother handed her a sandwich, which she opened. The ham inside must have pleased her, because she ate it. As they always did, Alice and Carrie traded halves of their sandwiches.

"Yours looks delicious," Mother exclaimed to Alice. "I can see that it is made with your mother's fantastic whole wheat bread. But what is inside?"

"Cucumbers, cream cheese and alfalfa sprouts."

Carrie gave her mother a bite. "Do you want a bite?" she asked Kate. "Alice's mother makes the best sandwiches in the whole world."

Kate looked at the sandwich and turned away without saying anything.

When they had finished the sandwiches, Alice brought out a bag of cookies and placed it in the middle of the blanket. "Health cookies for everyone," she announced.

"Your mother is amazing." Carrie's mother sighed. "Five children, a big house, a huge garden, and still she bakes bread and cookies."

"She doesn't work like you do, Mrs. Clark."

"There you are wrong, Alice. Your mother doesn't go out to a paying job like I do, but she works. Believe me, she works." Mother handed a cookie to Kate. "They're delicious."

"Health cookies," sneered Kate. "Who wants cookies to be healthy? Give me chocolate chip any time."

"These are just as good as chocolate chip," said Alice. "They have dates in them, and wheat germ and oatmeal. My mother . . ."

Kate got up and walked away from them down to the water.

"It's so hot today and it will be even hotter at

home, but I guess we'd better get going," Mother announced after they had been lying on the beach in silence for a time. "Maybe we'll go to the library today. It's air-conditioned. Then we'll buy you some sneakers, Carrie, and do the grocery shopping. Did you walk to the beach, Alice? I'll drive you home."

"Thanks, Mrs. Clark." Alice was looking intently at Kate's back. When she turned and caught Carrie's eye, Alice shrugged her shoulders. Carrie answered her with a shrug.

Carrie and her mother hung the wet towels on the line in the backyard, and then Carrie went upstairs to take off her bathing suit. Glancing out of the window, she saw Kate rolling her bike out of the garage, a baseball mitt hung over the handlebars.

"Hey, Kate," Carrie called. "Where are you going?"

The only answer Kate gave was to swing onto her bike and pedal off at top speed. Carrie might have run after her except that she was naked. By the time she was dressed, Kate was out of sight.

"Hey, Mother," Carrie called, running down the stairs. "Where has Kate gone?"

"What do you mean, where has Kate gone?"

"She rode out of here on her bike with a baseball mitt."

"I suppose we can deduce that she has gone to play baseball." Mother paused. "I'll just step next door and see if Paul is gone. They were on the raft together this morning. They may have made plans then."

"But she didn't ask if she could go."

"No." Mother sighed and started across the lawn.

"Shall I ride down to the field and tell Kate to come home?"

"No. You stay right where you are."

When Mother returned, she said that Paul had gone to play baseball, in spite of the heat. Danny, too.

"I thought we were going to the library," said Carrie, feeling cross and left out.

"I thought so, too. Do you have a book to tide you over?" Carrie nodded. "Then we'll just spend a quiet afternoon at home. I'll phone Daddy and ask him to stop for bread and milk. Why don't you go make us some lemonade, old dear, and then bring your book out to the porch where it's cool, or at least as cool as it is anyplace?"

Carrie made the lemonade and brought the icy glasses to the porch. Then she went upstairs to get her book, which was lying on her desk beside the list she had made on Saturday. Three pages of things she and her "sister" could do together. Carrie ripped the pages down the middle and then kept on tearing them into smaller and smaller pieces. Somehow the tearing made her feel better, and she spent a quiet afternoon with *The Witch of Blackbird Pond*. Mother, she noticed, spent much of the afternoon looking at her watch.

When Daddy got home, he and Mother went to the kitchen together, and Carrie could not hear a sound, which meant that they were whispering. Carrie tried to concentrate on her book but she could not. What were they going to do to Kate? Maybe they would ask Uncle Richard to come take her home. Truth to tell, Carrie liked that idea. Maybe they would ground Kate. Carrie liked that idea even better. If she didn't have any place to go or anyone else to see, Kate might play games. She might at least talk.

Carrie was setting the table when Kate finally rode into the driveway. Her beautiful golden hair was streaked with sweat and her face and clothes were dirty.

Daddy and Mother were waiting on the porch.

"Go take a shower and then come right down here," Daddy said.

Carrie finished the table and went and sat on the steps. If she sat on the porch in full view of her parents, they might send her away. At last she heard Kate's steps.

"Can I use your hair dryer?" she asked as she came onto the porch.

"Yes," said Mother in a tight voice. "But first we want to talk with you. Where have you been this afternoon?"

"Playing baseball." There was surprise in Kate's voice.

"Why didn't you ask Aunt Joan if you could go?" Daddy asked.

"Ask Aunt Joan?" Kate repeated.

"Yes, ask Aunt Joan," said Daddy firmly. "You are a member of this family this summer; as such, we expect you to abide by our rules. One of the rules is this: Children must ask before they go anyplace out of the yard. Please don't misunderstand. We have no objection to your playing baseball. But we must know where you are."

"Actually," added Mother, "it's a rule that applies to all of us. Uncle Rob and I never go away without telling Carrie where we will be. If we get held up, we phone her. The hair dryer is in the linen closet. We'll be eating dinner in about fifteen minutes."

That was all. Carrie was disappointed. If she'd gone off without asking, she'd have been punished. So they were treating Kate like a guest after all.

At dinner, Daddy asked about the game. No, it wasn't Little League, just two teams that played most afternoons. No, there weren't any other girls, but the catcher on Paul's team had gone to camp for two weeks, so Paul had said she could play. Daddy also asked Carrie about her day, but Carrie had very little to report, having spent the whole afternoon reading.

"You may clear the table, Kate," Mother said after dinner. "Carrie will load the dishwasher."

So they weren't treating Kate exactly like a guest.

4

Tuesday was just like Monday, except that the girls rode their bikes to their swimming lessons and came home for lunch. Kate on her ten-speed racer rode far ahead of Carrie on her three-speed girl's bike. Kate spent the morning at the raft and the afternoon playing baseball. Carrie spent the morning on the beach and the afternoon reading. She finished *The Witch of Blackbird Pond* and started *The Summer of the Swans*.

"I'm down to my last book," she announced at dinner.

"Oh dear," wailed Mother in mock sympathy. "When Carrie gets down to her last book, she's like a man lost in the desert, who is down to his last teaspoon of water. She panics," Mother explained to Kate. "There is only one remedy—a trip to the library. Think you can give up baseball for one afternoon?"

Kate hung her head and frowned. "Team needs me," she finally mumbled.

"I'm sure they do," said Mother. "But we need you too. We go to Pittsfield to the library, and that's fifteen miles away. We'll also do the shopping for the next week or two. It's beginning to look like Mother Hubbard's cupboard around here. And Carrie needs a new pair of sneakers. All that will take the whole afternoon. I don't want to leave you here alone."

Kate didn't say anything until they were in bed that night. For the first time, she spoke after the light was turned off.

"Your mother treats us like babies," she said. "My mother wouldn't have made me go to Pittsfield."

"Your mother . . ." Carrie stopped herself. She was about to remind Kate that her mother had left her.

"What were you going to say about my mother?" Kate demanded.

"Nothing. Just that your mother is not my mother."

"How clever of you to notice," Kate sneered. She flopped down on the mattress so hard that the room shook.

Carrie and her mother chatted happily during the ride to Pittsfield. Kate said nothing. Carrie and her mother each took out an armload of books from the Pittsfield library. Kate was finally persuaded to check out two books. Carrie and her mother shopped for sneakers and food. Kate insisted on staying in the car, although it was brutally hot. Kate remained silent all through supper.

"Let's play croquet," Daddy suggested while they were eating their ice cream. "There seems to be a slight breeze out back. We'll play partners. Kate and I will take on Carrie and Mother. OK?"

Kate didn't say anything, but he set up the wickets while the girls loaded the dishwasher.

"Do you like croquet?" Carrie asked, trying to make conversation.

"Not particularly."

Carrie couldn't think of another thing to say, so the only sound was the clicking of mallets against balls as Mother and Daddy took practice shots around the lawn.

Kate went first, and she had just finished her turn and was already headed for the center wicket when Paul and Danny came through the hedge that separated their yard from the Clarks' yard.

"We lost the game today because you weren't there." Paul sounded as if he were accusing Kate of a terrible crime.

"Did you? What was the score? I'll be there tomorrow. Were there any home runs?" Kate smiled happily at Paul.

"I was the catcher," announced Danny. Danny was a year younger than Carrie and two years younger than his brother.

"Who played shortstop then?" asked Kate.

"Nobody."

"Want to play croquet with us?" asked Daddy.

The brothers picked up mallets and formed a partnership. Throughout the game Kate made noises Carrie had never heard from her before. She shouted encouragement and groaned with dismay. Although she had just said that she didn't particularly like croquet, she threw herself into the game with enthusiasm.

Kate and Daddy won.

"That's enough for me," Daddy announced. "I want to quit while I'm ahead."

"Me too," said Mother. "I'll quit while I'm behind."

"Let's play another game," Kate suggested. "We'll play the oldest against the youngest."

"Paul's the oldest and I'm the youngest," said Danny. "So who do I get to play with?"

"I'm three months older than Carrie." Kate sounded as if that were something to be proud of. "So Paul and I will play you and Carrie."

"That's not fair," both Carrie and Danny said together, but they shrugged their shoulders and picked up their mallets. They did the best they could, which turned out not to be so bad—not winning but not disgraceful either.

Actually, it was fun because it turned dark before the game was over, and they finished the game by flashlight. Paul got through the wickets first.

"I'm going to go after the little kids and knock

them out of the way while you finish," he called to Kate. "Hold the light over Danny's ball."

He made a mighty swing, and his ball missed its target by less than an inch and rolled into the flower bed. Then they all had to look with flashlights until they finally found it nestled among the zinnias. Still the game continued as the court grew darker and the shots grew wilder. Daddy and Mother stood on the porch and watched.

Mother had sodas ready for them when the game ended. Paul and Kate sat on the porch steps and talked about baseball. Danny joined them. Carrie too. They were talking a language she didn't understand, about people she'd never heard of. Still the soda was cold and refreshing, and it was nice to hear Kate's voice. She sounded relaxed and happy and unlike the girl who had gone to Pittsfield with them just a few hours earlier.

"I'm glad you like my friends," Carrie said that night after the light was out.

"I like Paul and Danny, but not that scrawny little health-nut friend of yours."

"Alice is my best friend."

"To each his own," said Kate.

Nothing was working out as Carrie had planned. Her "sister" didn't want to talk with her, much less play games. She cluttered Carrie's room. So far she hadn't put a thing in any of the drawers that had

been emptied for her or hung anything in the closet. Most of her clothes were still in the suitcase. Everything else was lying in heaps around the room. Kate was sloppy, gloomy, unfriendly. Carrie was cross.

She told Alice about it at the beach.

"So why don't you just ignore her?" Alice suggested. "Come on over to my house this afternoon. I'm in charge of the baby afternoons during the summer, but he takes a long nap."

Carrie liked to visit Alice. She lived in an old yellow farmhouse that always smelled good—woodburning fires and baking bread in the winter, pickles and ripe fruit in the summer. The Rileys had two dogs, three or more cats, chickens and a pig. They also had rows of fruit trees and a huge garden. The most interesting feature of their home, however, was Peter.

Last summer Carrie had watched as Mrs. Riley's stomach had grown larger and larger, until she could hardly lift herself out of a chair. Then one morning Alice had called at seven o'clock to announce that the baby had been born. She had wanted a girl, but she got a boy and his name was Peter. When he was six days old, Alice had invited Carrie to come and meet him.

Looking at that little tiny baby was awesome. She stood, just staring at him. Then, without a word of warning, Mrs. Riley put Peter into Carrie's arms. Carrie couldn't say a word. She carefully backed toward a chair and sat down. His tiny ears and fingernails were perfect. She loosened the blanket around him and looked at his toes and his skinny feet. He opened his dark blue eyes and stared at her. Then his face had wrinkled up and he had begun to cry. He made a surprisingly loud sound for such a tiny baby.

Mrs. Riley took him from Carrie and put him to her breast. Carrie had turned away, embarrassed at seeing Alice's mother's breast exposed.

"You can look," Alice had said in her matter-of-fact way. Carrie had looked. In fact, in the following months, she had watched the baby nurse so many times that it became boring, but that first time she had felt a kind of welling-up joy she had never known before.

"Does it hurt?" she had whispered.

"Of course not." Alice knew a lot about babies.

"I don't know how to describe nursing a baby to you girls," Mrs. Riley had said. "It's wonderful. It makes me feel all peaceful. At the same time, it is exciting."

"And it's good for the baby," added Alice.

All year long Carrie had watched Peter grow and learn. Now he was almost a year old. He was taking his nap when Carrie arrived on her bike soon after lunch. She tiptoed upstairs to look at him sleeping in his crib with his knees pulled up under him and his little diapered bottom sticking up in the air.

Then she and Alice made a thermos of lemonade and packed a bag of cookies and climbed up into the maple tree in the yard just outside Peter's window. They each found a comfortable fork in the branches

33

and ate and drank and enjoyed what few breezes ruffled the leaves.

Unlike Carrie's plans, Alice's plans for the summer were all working out. The Rileys were going to open a roadside stand. They would sell vegetables from their garden. Alice was learning to make bread so she could sell that.

"I could help you make bread," Carrie said, "if I knew how."

"Want to learn? We'll ask my mother to teach you. Then you can sell your bread at our stand too."

The girls discussed their bread and the money they would make until Peter called. Then they went inside and Alice changed his diapers and Carrie carried him to the kitchen. Mrs. Riley was shelling peas and listening to the radio.

"I have just discovered that Mozart wrote perfect pea-shelling music," she announced.

"Would you teach me to make bread while you are teaching Alice?" Carrie asked.

"Of course. That's a great idea. You'll like making bread, Carrie. It's more fun than any other kind of cooking. It's too hot to bake bread now, but we'll start on the first cool day."

Peter, who had been sitting on the floor beside his mother, pulled himself to a standing position, holding on to his mother's chair. He walked around the chair, holding on with one hand.

"Why don't you let go and walk across the room?" Alice asked, holding out her hands to him. "You look strong enough to me. Come on, Peter, come to Alice."

Peter laughed and continued to walk around his mother's chair.

"Come on, Peter," Carrie coaxed, copying Alice's voice. "Come to Carrie." She picked up a pea pod and held it out to him. He reached for it with his free hand. Then he reached for it with his other hand. Then he took a step toward it. And another. Carrie grabbed him as he started to fall.

"His first steps," Mrs. Riley crooned. "And he took them to you, Carrie. I've always known you were very special to Peter."

Could that be true—or was it just the pretty green pea pod? Peter had a mother and a father and four brothers and sisters, and everybody loved him. Carrie loved him too. Did he know that? She picked him up and hugged him and then put him back on his feet. He walked to Alice and then back to Carrie.

During dinner Carrie told her parents about Peter's first steps and about the bread-baking project.

"Now that's what I call a constructive plan," said Mother. "Just wait, Rob, until you taste homemade bread à la the Rileys."

"I'm going to sell my bread at the Rileys' vegetable stand."

"Oh no, you're not." Mother shook her finger at Carrie in mock anger. "You're going to sell it to me. In the meantime, ladies"—Mother looked at Carrie and then at Kate—"I want to remind you that Friday, tomorrow, is cleaning day at the Clarks'."

"And Saturday is gardening day," added Daddy.

Mother assigned tasks. The girls were to clean their room and change the sheets. Carrie was to dust all of the furniture downstairs and vacuum the carpeting. Kate was to vacuum the wood floors and sweep the porch.

"And, Kate," Mother added. "Please put your things away in the drawers we have provided for your use. Then you can put your suitcase under the bed. You'll look and feel more settled if it is out of the way."

Kate didn't say anything.

"Perhaps you'd rather move into my sewing room. There are some empty drawers in the chest in there. Would you prefer to sleep there?"

"I don't care," said Kate.

"Well, you decide and settle someplace." Mother rose from the table and gave Kate a hug.

5

It was dark in Carrie's room when she awoke the next morning. At first she thought it was still night. Then she heard raindrops tapping on the roof. She reached down and pulled the quilt up over her and snuggled into it.

"Isn't it glorious?" Mother said, coming to their door. "You've both slept late. Get up and I'll make you pancakes, and then we'll start our chores. It's a perfect cleaning day."

The phone rang while they were eating breakfast. Carrie answered it.

"That was Alice. It's bread-baking day," she announced happily as she returned to the table. "They're going to be ready to begin in about an hour. You're invited too, Kate. Will you drive us, Mother?"

"I'll drive and you can do your downstairs chores when you get home, but I want that room cleaned before you leave."

Carrie jumped up and put her plate in the dishwasher. "Come on, Kate."

"I'm not going." Kate got up from the table and walked out onto the porch.

Carrie looked at her mother, who looked away. She ran upstairs, stripped the sheets off her bed and put them with her dirty clothes in the hamper. Then she started to make up the bed with clean sheets. She had expected Kate to come and help her. Mother came instead. When the bed was made, she stacked her library books neatly on the shelves and put away the few things that were hers on the dresser. The room was still a mess but it was not Carrie's mess.

"I can't vacuum this room," she called to Mother.

"Then go dust downstairs. Kate will vacuum when she has picked up her things." Mother sounded cross.

When the dusting was done, Mother told Kate, who was still sitting on the porch, that she would be back in a few minutes. She and Carrie put on their raincoats and ran to the garage.

"I hope Kate does move into your sewing room," Carrie announced as they drove out of the garage. "She's unfriendly and sloppy, and she won't do any of the things I had planned."

"She's troubled and unhappy, and we'll be patient and hope that things will get better," Mother said firmly. Then she smiled over at Carrie. "I know it's been tough, old dear, but just keep on trying. Please."

Carrie smiled back. She was still smiling when she ran into the Rileys' kitchen.

"Hi, Carrie," Mrs. Riley greeted her. "I thought your cousin was coming with you."

"She's not." That sounded too blunt but Carrie couldn't think of anything else to say.

"Why?" asked Alice.

"Mother says she's troubled."

"Then it's especially too bad she didn't come," said Mrs. Riley. "Bread making is a wonderful way to relieve tensions. Remember that, girls. If you ever feel angry or upset, go to the kitchen and start baking bread." She had set three huge bowls on the big oval kitchen table. "First we'll test the yeast." She handed each girl a cake of yeast and kept one herself. "Put one-half cup lukewarm water in your bowl and crumble the yeast into it. Add one tablespoon honey and stir until the yeast is dissolved."

While they were doing that, she told them that when they saw bubbles on top of the water, they would know that the yeast was going to do its job, which was to make the dough rise. All they actually needed to make bread was more water and flour. To make this bread as tasty and nutritious as possible, they would add dried milk, shortening, soy flour, wheat germ, and an egg.

Just as Mrs. Riley had said, bubbles began to appear in the water in their bowls. They added all of the other ingredients and stirred. Then they added more flour, and more flour, and more flour. When the mixture was too stiff to stir, they put it out onto floured boards.

"Now we start to get rid of all of our aggressions," Mrs. Riley said as she folded the sticky dough toward her, sprinkled it with more flour, and pressed it with the heel of her hand. The girls did the same. Fold. Press. Fold. Press. Sprinkle with flour. Fold. Press. . . . Finally the sticky dough wasn't sticky anymore but a smooth mass.

"Just like a baby's bottom," Mrs. Riley said, giving her dough a couple of sharp smacks. "Wonder why my kids are so great?" she asked Carrie. "It's because I'm such an expert spanker."

She gave her dough another three spanks. Carrie and Alice spanked their dough, too. Then they washed their bowls, dried them and buttered them. They put the rounds of dough into the bowls, turned them so there was butter on top of the dough and covered them with clean towels.

"That's it, ladies. Clean up the flour you've sprinkled around, and we'll have lunch while the dough is rising. Oatmeal bread," she said as she took out a loaf and began to slice. "That comes in a later lesson."

Mrs. Riley went to the door and blew a whistle, and the family appeared. After lunch, Alice took Peter upstairs and put him to bed, and everyone else disappeared again. The bread makers loaded the dishwasher and checked their bowls. The balls of dough that had nestled in the bottoms of the bowls had swollen into large mounds.

Mrs. Riley made a fist and then she began to growl.

"Take that," she said as she punched her fist into the top of the dough. As if frightened, the dough began to shrink.

"Take that," said Alice.

"Pow," said Carrie.

They shaped their dough into loaves and put it into bread pans, nine loaves in all. They buttered the tops of their loaves and covered them with towels.

"OK, ladies, we'll set the timer for one hour. It may be ready to bake then."

Alice and Carrie went up to the room Alice shared with her sister. They set up the backgammon board, but they talked more than they played. When they returned to the kitchen, their loaves had risen above the sides of the pans.

"I've already preheated the oven," Mrs. Riley said, "but if you bake bread at home, Carrie, you must start the oven about fifteen minutes before you think your bread will be ready to bake." They put all their loaves into the huge oven. "Now I think I'll phone your mother, Carrie, and suggest that she and your cousin come over in about an hour to eat warm-from-the-oven home-baked bread."

The nine loaves of bread that stood cooling on wire racks were smooth, golden and beautiful. They were like magnets drawing every member of the Riley family into the kitchen. Mrs. Riley sent each of the newcomers away, saying that the bread was still too hot to cut. Peter woke, as if he too wanted a slice of warm bread, and Alice and Carrie brought him to the kitchen.

"I'm going to start drooling any minute now if I don't get a slice of bread," Alice announced as she put a plate of butter and a big dish of strawberry jam in the center of the table.

As soon as Mother drove into the driveway, Mrs. Riley poured boiling water over herbal leaves in the large teapot. Kate was with Mother, much to Carrie's surprise. Mother introduced her to Mrs. Riley, who welcomed her with a hug, which Kate received stiffly. They all sat down at the big table, and Mrs. Riley cut thick slices of bread.

"Heavenly," pronounced Mother.

Carrie picked up Peter and gave him a small piece of bread.

"Muh, muh," said Peter.

"He's saying *more*," interpreted Alice.

Carrie gave him another piece.

"You're a darling," Mother said and held out her hands to the baby, who went to her with a smile, as if he quite agreed.

One by one, the other members of the Riley family came in and sat down at the table to eat bread and drink tea. Outside it was still raining but inside it was sunny and warm.

When it was time to leave, Mrs. Riley put Carrie's loaves in a paper bag and told her to wait until they were completely cool to wrap them tightly in plastic bags.

"Disgusting," said Kate as they drove away from the Rileys' house.

"What's disgusting?" asked Carrie.

"The Rileys."

"What's disgusting about the Rileys?" Mother sounded shocked; Carrie *was* shocked.

"You'd think they'd never heard of the population explosion or women's lib. Five children. My mother says it is sinful to have more than two children in this day and age. And look at Mrs. Riley. Women should use their talents, not waste them baking bread and looking after children who should never have been born!"

Carrie waited for her mother to say something. She didn't. She just drove on, gripping the steering wheel. Well, if her mother wouldn't speak, she, Carrie, would tell that Kate a thing or two. "What does your mother know. . . ."

"Carrie, be still," Mother commanded in her I-will-be-obeyed voice. She pulled into the driveway, stopped the car and turned off the motor. She took a deep breath.

"But if the Rileys had only two children, Alice would never have been born," wailed Carrie. "Alice is a wonderful person. She deserved to be born."

"That's true," said Mother in her let's-all-bereasonable voice. "But I'm sure that Kate was talking about general principles, not individual people. As a general principle, one might say that couples should have no more children than they can provide for. I can assure you, Kate, that the Riley children are well provided for. Furthermore, they all seem to be particularly bright and kind, and I'd be willing to bet that they will grow into fine, useful adults."

"And Alice's parents love her," inserted Carrie.

Mother gave Carrie's knee a tap, which meant *keep quiet.* Then she continued her lecture. "As for the principles of women's liberation, Kate, Mrs. Riley is an unusually talented mother and homemaker, and she seems to enjoy what she is doing. Maybe she'd also be a terrific business executive or truck driver, but if she wants to raise children and bake bread, why shouldn't she?"

"But those children are using up the world's resources."

"They're not even doing much of that. The Rileys raise much of their own food. They even burn wood from their own land to heat their house, except when it is very cold." Mother didn't sound at all angry anymore.

"You don't have lots of children, and you work," said Kate. "So you must agree with my mother. My mother has an exciting job in New York. She's a terrific artist, you know. She has to fulfill herself. She can't be tied to a house and family." Before either Carrie or her mother could say another word, Kate had jumped out of the backseat and run into the house.

"That was a terrible thing for Kate to say about the Rileys," Carrie said as Mother started the car's motor and drove into the garage.

"It was, or it would have been if Kate had been talking about the Rileys, but she wasn't."

"What do you mean?"

"I mean that Kate is loyal and that she loves her mother and wants to believe that her mother was right in moving away."

"Do you think Aunt Janet was right?"

"That's not for me to say."

"Would you like to have five children and bake bread?" Carrie asked.

"No, I would not. I'm quite happy with one daughter. Frankly, Carrie, I am a very good teacher and I like my work. I am not an enthusiastic housecleaner or cook. In other words, I'd rather spend my day in the classroom than at home. Besides, we've got a bread baker in the family now, and one is enough. Was it fun baking bread?"

Carrie told her mother about relieving tensions and slapping the baby's bottom. They both laughed at that.

"I wish we could find something to help relieve Kate's tensions," Mother said.

"Maybe that's why she likes baseball. Maybe hitting a ball is like kneading bread."

"Maybe it is."

6

While Carrie had been at the Rileys', Kate had cleaned their room and put away her suitcase. She had obviously decided not to move to the sewing room.

The next morning, the sky was clear and they all four spent the morning doing garden and yard work. In the afternoon, Kate played baseball and Carrie read a book.

The second week of Kate's stay started like the first. Carrie learned to make whole wheat bread. Kate hit a homer. Carrie sometimes thought about all the plans she had made for the summer, when she would have a "sister." They had all "gang aft a-gley," as Dad would say. Kate was flying hair far ahead of her on the road to the beach; a silent figure sitting at the dinner table across from her; a mound in the other bed in her room. Nothing more.

Carrie's relationship with Ebony the cat was more

fun than her relationship with Kate, her cousin. Ebony seemed to like her. Kate acted as if she didn't exist.

Thursday night, for one moment, Carrie was able to hope that the relationship might improve. Kate began to talk after they went to bed.

"You have a sleeping bag?" Kate asked to open the conversation.

"Yes. Sometimes Mother and Daddy and I go camping. Last summer we went to Maine. Did you ever go camping?"

"No."

"Maybe we could all four go together sometime this summer. You'd like to camp. I know you would."

"Maybe," said Kate. "May I borrow your sleeping bag this weekend?"

"Why?" asked Carrie.

"None of your business."

So much for an improving relationship, thought Carrie. "I'm not going to lend it to you unless you tell me why you want it," she said.

"OK, Miss Nosy. I'm going camping with the team."

"Did my folks say you can go?"

"I haven't asked them. Why should I? They aren't my parents."

"But you still have to tell them before you go away."

"I'll leave a note if you insist." Neither girl said anything for a few minutes.

"So where's the sleeping bag?" Kate demanded. "It isn't in the closet."

"No, we keep all of our camping gear . . ." Carrie stopped. "I'll get it for you when I've heard one of my parents say that you may go. Not until then."

Kate didn't say a word about camping all during the day on Friday. Then when dinner was over and the girls were beginning to clear the table, Kate glared at Carrie.

"I'm going camping tomorrow night," she called over her shoulder as she carried a stack of dirty plates into the kitchen.

"Come back here, Kate," Mother called after her.

When Kate had put the plates down and returned to the dining room, Mother asked her to sit down and tell them all about it, who was going where.

"The team. We're going to ride our bikes to a campground Paul knows about beside a lake in Pittsfield."

"That sounds like fun," said Daddy. "What adults are going?"

"I don't know."

"Are any adults going?" asked Mother.

"I don't know."

"Come off it, Kate," said Daddy. "You must know if there will be any adults going on this trip. You must

50

also know that it is a simple matter for us to find out from Paul's parents."

"OK. We're going by ourselves."

"Any other girls planning to go?"

"There aren't any other girls on the team." Kate got up to take another load to the kitchen.

Carrie saw Mother shake her head at Daddy.

"Come back, Kate," called Daddy. "I'm sorry, really sorry, but I cannot allow you to go on an overnight trip without chaperones."

"But . . ."

"There are no buts. You may not go."

"You're not my parents," Kate muttered.

"That's true, but we are acting for your parents. Richard told me to treat you just as we would treat Carrie. We would definitely not allow Carrie to go on this trip, and we're not allowing you to go either."

Kate scowled, banged the dishes as she put them in the dishwasher, and then went upstairs.

"Stay away," she shouted when Carrie started to follow her.

Kate scowled all day Saturday. In the morning they weeded the tomatoes and beans, and Kate attacked each weed as if she hated it individually.

"You've done a terrific job, girls," Daddy said when he came to check on their work. "How would you like to watch the Yankee game on television this afternoon, Kate?"

Kate didn't answer, but she and Daddy watched

the game. Daddy shouted words of encouragement to his favorite players. Kate scowled, turning away from the set occasionally to glare at Daddy.

In the evening they all went to the movies. Carrie knew that her folks were trying to make Kate happy. They were not successful. Kate was still scowling on Sunday. Sunday night they went out for hamburgers.

When they came home, Kate went over to Paul and Danny's. Carrie went with her. It had been a terrific trip, the boys said. They talked on and on about how much fun they had had. Carrie kept trying to change the subject; Kate couldn't have enjoyed hearing every single detail of a trip she had missed.

"By the way, Kate, Jerry's back," Paul said. "He went with us. Sorry."

Kate turned and ran back to the Clark house.

"What's that about?" Carrie asked Danny.

"Jerry's our catcher. We won't be needing Kate on the team anymore. At least not until somebody else goes on vacation."

"But Kate likes to play and she's good. You said so yourself."

"Yeah, but we guys stick together."

"Male chauvinist pig," Carrie shouted and ran home after Kate.

She ran right up to their bedroom. Kate was there but the door was closed. When Carrie knocked, Kate told her to go away and stay away.

Carrie went downstairs and told her parents what had happened.

"Oh, dear." There were tears in Mother's voice. "Poor Kate. What are we going to do for her? What can we do?"

"Maybe you should ask the boys to let her play?" Carrie suggested.

"Kate wouldn't like that and neither would the boys. They might let her play, but it wouldn't be the same," said Daddy.

They sat in silence. Carrie tried to think of things they could do that would please Kate, but Kate didn't like her plans. Kate didn't like her. The truth was, Carrie didn't like Kate either. Nevertheless, she felt very, very sorry for her.

Mother worked the puzzle in the Sunday *Times*, or pretended to work it. Daddy read the sports section, or pretended to read it. Carrie leafed through an issue of *Seventeen* without even seeing the pictures. They were all three surprised when Kate suddenly appeared with a big smile on her face.

"May I have a stamp, please?" she asked.

"Sure," said Daddy and went to get her one.

"Who'd you write to?" Carrie asked.

"Want to play a game?" Kate asked, ignoring Carrie's question.

"Sure." Carrie was so surprised, she could hardly remember what games they had.

"I'd like to play Clue," said Mother.

And that's what they did. They all sat around the table in the kitchen playing Clue and drinking lemonade. It was the best evening they'd had since Kate had come to stay with them.

Monday morning Kate waited for Carrie, and the girls rode together to the post office to mail Kate's letter before they went on to the beach. Kate ignored Carrie's questions about the letter, and she kept the address hidden, but she was not nasty about it.

After her lesson, Kate offered to teach Alice to swim. "You just need to get over your fear," Kate said. "In your head you know that the water will hold you up."

"But my heart says that it's just waiting to pull me down to the bottom of the lake." Alice shuddered.

"I will keep my hand on your arm so you will know I am right beside you," Kate said reasonably. With Kate's hand on her arm, Alice was soon floating and kicking.

Monday afternoon they played games, and Monday evening Paul and Danny came over to play croquet. Tuesday it rained, and Kate and Carrie and Paul and Danny played Monopoly all day long. It was just as much fun as Carrie had hoped it would be. Tuesday night Aunt Janet phoned, and she and Kate talked a long, long time. Kate returned to the living room to announce proudly that her mother's design was going to be used on a new line of sheets and pillowcases.

7

The next day, Wednesday, Kate gave Alice another swimming lesson. Alice learned to move her arms. She even learned to breathe and swim at the same time—if Kate was right beside her with her hand touching any part of Alice's body.

On Thursday, Kate took a long stick into the water. Alice started swimming with Kate's hand on her shoulder. Then Kate put just a finger on her, then the stick. Alice laughed when she stopped swimming and saw that it had been a stick that had been making her feel so confident. From then on, it was enough to have Kate swimming beside her.

Friday they walked out into the water until it was up to Alice's shoulder.

"We'll swim here today," Kate announced. "I'll swim on the deep side, but you know that any time you want to stop, you will be able to put your feet on the bottom of the lake and your head will be above water. You know that, don't you?"

Alice nodded in agreement and swam back and forth between the ropes.

"We were wrong about your cousin," Alice announced to Carrie later that morning. "She's a nice person."

Carrie agreed. After two weeks in which even the air they breathed at home had seemed strange, everything was almost normal. Her house felt right again. Her parents were behaving like themselves. Carrie was enjoying the summer.

"I've got a terrific idea," she announced. "Kate wanted to go camping with the boys on the team, and my folks wouldn't let her, so let's do this: Let's go for a long bike ride, then to the beach, and then to my house, where we'll put up the tent and pretend to be camping in the woods. We'll cook our dinner outside and sleep in the tent. Let's do it tomorrow."

"Great scheme!" responded Alice.

She described a hamburger stew they could cook in foil over the coals. She would bring all the vegetables. Carrie would supply the hamburger. As soon as Kate came out of the water, they rushed to tell her their plan.

"Sorry," said Kate. "I won't be able to go."

"Why not?" Carrie and Alice asked in unison.

"My father is coming tomorrow to take me home."

Carrie stared at her cousin. Kate had come for the summer, the whole summer, not just three weeks. That's what her folks had said. They hadn't mentioned that Kate was going home.

"Do my folks know?" she finally asked.

"No. I just wrote to Daddy on Sunday night. I told him to come and get me this weekend."

"But my swimming lessons," wailed Alice. "I'll never learn to swim if you aren't here to teach me. Please stay, Kate. Maybe the Clarks would let you phone him to say you'd changed your mind."

"Sorry." Kate did not sound the least bit sorry. "Besides, you already know how to swim. You just need practice. Carrie can swim with you."

"But she couldn't save me if the lake started to pull me down."

"How many times do I have to tell you that the water holds you up? Carrie could at least call for help if you needed it. She has a big mouth. I have to go pack."

Kate strode off toward her bike and rode away.

"So much for that scheme," said Carrie. "I guess if Uncle Richard is going to be here, I'd better stay home. We'll camp another weekend. OK?"

"OK," agreed Alice.

While they were eating their sandwiches at the kitchen table, Carrie asked her mother if she knew that Uncle Richard was coming to get Kate.

"What are you talking about?" Mother sounded as if Carrie had just announced a weekend trip to the moon.

"I guess I should have told you that my father is

coming this weekend to take me home," Kate said sweetly.

"We haven't heard from him, Kate. Have you?"

"No. But I wrote to him on Sunday and mailed it on Monday. When do you think he would get my letter?"

"Wednesday, maybe Thursday. But I think he'd phone before he came, don't you?"

"Maybe. Maybe he'll call tonight."

Kate went upstairs and started packing. Mother phoned Daddy at the plant. Daddy tried to phone Uncle Richard right after dinner. He tried again later in the evening. And again. No one answered.

"Maybe he left after work and will get here in the night," suggested Kate.

"Look, Kate." Daddy stopped and sighed. "Maybe your father didn't get your letter. Maybe he's out of town. I know he planned for you to stay all summer. We had hoped you'd stay. We really like having you here, you know."

"Thank you," said Kate very formally. "Daddy needs me to cook his dinners and keep the house clean. I've had a very nice vacation, but it is time for me to go home. I told him so in my letter. He'll be here tomorrow."

Saturday was such a hot, muggy day that Daddy did not make them weed very long. Carrie suggested that they ride to the beach to cool off, but Kate said she had to stick around to be there when her father arrived. "He might want to go right back this afternoon," she explained.

Kate took a shower and put on a shorts and top set that Carrie had never seen before. Then she brought her suitcase and shopping bags downstairs and lined them up neatly beside the front door.

Carrie saw her mother watching Kate. Then Daddy came and patted Mother's shoulder. Mother looked like she might burst into tears. Kate sat on the porch steps until lunchtime.

"I have a good idea," Daddy said. His phony cheerful voice had returned, Carrie noticed. "The living room is as cool as any place today. I'll bring down the fan from our bedroom and we'll watch the Mets game. I'll drink beer and you can drink lemonade. How about it?" Kate didn't say anything. "Look, honey, you can see the driveway from the living room window," he said gently.

"OK," said Kate.

Carrie and her mother sat on the porch and read while Kate and Daddy watched the game. They could hear Daddy's voice shouting "What a hit! Did you see that catch? Come on, Mets!"

"Poor Daddy." Mother sighed. "He's trying so hard to keep Kate diverted."

It was then that Carrie realized that her parents didn't expect Uncle Richard to come. Poor Kate. What if her father didn't show up?

As soon as the game was over, Carrie suggested

that they play Mastermind. "We can play on the porch. You can see the driveway from there."

Kate agreed, but neither of them could concentrate.

"We could invite Paul and Danny over for croquet this evening," Carrie suggested.

"My father will be here by then," Kate said, as if daring Carrie to refute her statement.

"Of course," Carrie agreed.

But Uncle Richard did not come. Kate jumped every time a car came down the street or the telephone rang. It was never her father. They played games all evening.

"It's long past bedtime," Daddy finally announced. "Let's all turn in."

"I'll just wait up for Daddy," Kate said.

"No, Kate. We'll leave the front door unlocked tonight and a light on. If your father comes late, he can let himself in and go up to the sewing room and get some sleep. Then you can see him in the morning."

"But . . ."

"No buts, Kate. We're all going to bed."

And they did. When Carrie awoke in the morning, Kate was already up. Carrie rushed to the sewing room. The bed had not been slept in. Kate was sitting in the kitchen eating cereal.

"I'm sorry about your father," Carrie said.

"He'll be here today," Kate said firmly. "Guess he couldn't make it yesterday. Maybe he had to mow the lawn."

"Sure," said Carrie, but she didn't believe it.

Kate absolutely refused to go to church with them. She was sitting on the porch when they returned, her bags still standing by the front door.

Sunday afternoon was just like Saturday, only hotter and muggier. Kate and Daddy watched another game. Carrie and her mother read.

"Let's go get our hamburgers," Daddy suggested when the game was over.

"You go," said Kate. "I'll wait here for Daddy."

"He's not coming this weekend, Kate," Daddy said softly. "Maybe he didn't get your letter."

Kate looked at her uncle as if she could not believe what she was hearing. Then she turned away. "I'll wait," she said.

"It's too hot for hamburgers," Mother said. "Why don't I just make up a big tuna salad. We'll eat it on the porch and then we'll play croquet. OK?"

Just as they were starting to eat, the phone rang. Kate, who was closest to the door, got to the phone first, but Daddy pushed her aside and answered it himself.

"Yes, Richard," they heard him say. "We've been waiting for you." There were a series of quiet spaces and an "Oh" from Daddy and then, "We'll be glad to see you whenever you come." Then an "Oh" that sounded pained. Then, "Do you really think that is best?" Then, "Here she is."

Kate's conversation was no more revealing. "Why didn't you come?" she asked. "But I've been waiting for you for two days." Then a long space of silence. "I don't want to look at a boarding school. . . . Please, Daddy. Let me live with you. . . ." Kate was crying. "Uncle Rob wouldn't let me go camping and the boys won't let me play baseball. . . . Oh, Daddy . . ." They heard the receiver go down and the sound of Kate's feet as she ran up the stairs.

Carrie herself was crying and so, she saw, was Mother.

"Richard has been at the shore all week. He just got Kate's letter when he got home," Daddy explained. "His company wants to transfer him to Tulsa. He's going to sell the house and go. He and Janet have decided to send Kate to boarding school next year. They've heard about Mountvale in Lenox. Richard has an appointment to take Kate to see it a week from next Friday. He'll come up then."

"But Kate wouldn't have a home to go to during vacations," said Carrie.

"Her mother is going to get a larger apartment. She'll go to New York for vacations or come to us." Daddy sounded very cool and matter-of-fact.

"Doesn't anybody care about Kate?" asked Carrie.

"Of course. Many people care about Kate. Both of her parents love her very much. They just don't love one another anymore. She isn't the first child to be a victim of divorce, you know. Besides, we all love her."

Yes, thought Carrie, she did love Kate.

After a while, Mother took a glass of lemonade up to Kate and was up there with her for a long time. When Carrie finally went to bed, Kate was asleep.

8

Alice came running toward them across the sand as soon as they arrived at the beach the next day. "Oh, Kate," she shouted, "I'm glad you didn't go away. Now we can go camping next weekend."

Kate turned away from her and ran into the water. Carrie told Alice about their awful weekend.

The next day, Tuesday, Alice approached Kate with a neatly wrapped box with a card attached. "My mother asked me to give you these cookies to thank you for teaching me to swim," she said. "They're chocolate chip."

Kate said not a word. She took the box and dropped it on her towel and ran into the water. While the beginners were having their lesson, Kate came back to Alice.

"OK," she said, "let's get on with your lessons." Carrie followed along as they walked out to where the water was up to Alice's shoulders. "We'll swim to the raft today," Kate announced.

"But the water is too deep for me," Alice whispered.

"I'll touch you all the way," promised Kate.

"But . . ."

"Get going," ordered Kate.

"I . . ."

"You don't have to go if you don't want to," said Carrie. She did not like the sound of Kate's voice.

"Keep out of this, Carrie," Kate said.

"You promise to keep your hand on me?" asked Alice.

"Sure," promised Kate.

Alice started swimming with Kate touching her arm. Carrie swam after them. When they were in very deep water, Carrie saw that Kate was just touching Alice with the tip of her finger. Alice kept swimming. Good for Alice! There was a small splash and Kate was gone. She resurfaced yards closer to the raft.

"OK, mamma's little girl. Let's see you swim for your life. Remember you can't touch the bottom where you are now." Kate laughed an ugly laugh and turned on her back, moving swiftly away from them toward the raft.

Carrie swam the few strokes to Alice as fast as she could, but her friend had already gone under. She came up coughing and went down again. Carrie tried to reach her. She grabbed her bathing suit strap, but she could not bring Alice's head above water.

"Help," she shouted. "Help."

Within minutes it was all over. The swimming instructor reached them in a few strokes, pushed Carrie aside, grabbed Alice's chin and pulled her toward shore. Carrie, whose heart was throbbing in her chest so that she could scarcely breathe, treaded water and watched as Alice staggered through the shallow water to the beach.

Carrie was angry, angrier than she could ever remember being before. She swam on out to the raft, climbed up on it and stood over Kate.

"You're mean, Kate Clark. Mean, nasty, despicable, horrible. . . . Why did you do that to Alice?"

"She's such a mamma's baby. So are you. She's a fraidycat too. She was swimming all right when I left her."

"So why didn't you stay with her? I'll bet you'd planned that all along. You wanted to scare Alice. You don't like her. Why? Because her mother made you chocolate chip cookies? It's too bad about your mother, Kate, but that's no reason to be mean to Alice."

"What are you trying to say about my mother? If you have anything to say, Carrie, say it."

"Your mother left you. She just walked out and left. That's what I'm saying. You're mad because Alice's mother is happy staying at home."

"How do you know if she's happy? What would you know about anything?" Kate jumped up, dove into the water and swam ashore, far from where the other children had gathered around Alice. Carrie watched as Kate picked up her towel, kicked the box of cookies until it was buried in the sand, and got on her bike and rode off.

Then Carrie lay down on her stomach, her face in her arms, and cried.

"Are you all right?" Carrie hadn't seen the swimming instructor coming toward the raft, but there he was, sitting beside her. "The lessons are over now. Why don't we swim on in?"

"Thank you for saving Alice," Carrie sobbed. "She's my best friend, and I couldn't get her head above water."

"I know. But you called for help, and Alice is certainly OK. She's in better shape than you are. Come on now. Jump in."

Carrie jumped, and the instructor swam beside her until they were on shore.

"Wasn't that exciting?" Alice called to her. "I really swam in deep water. Next time I won't panic. Maybe I can skip intermediate and go right into advanced swimmers next year. Isn't that exciting?"

Alice's enthusiasm was too much for Carrie, who felt heavy and tired. She tried to smile at her friend. Then she dug the box of cookies out of the sand and read the note Mrs. Riley had written:

Dear Kate,

Thank you so much for helping Alice learn to swim. You've been so kind and we are all grateful. Alice said that you like chocolate chip cookies best of all.

Love,
Laura Riley

Carrie put the box in the basket on her bike and rode toward home slowly. *Would it never cool off?* She pushed her bike up a small hill that she usually pedaled. She felt weary, and weak and weepy. The bike wobbled as she turned into the driveway. Her mother was walking across the front lawn toward her.

"Hi. I've just been over to see Mrs. Cole. She's recovering very nicely from her fall. . . ." Mother stopped. "My goodness, Carrie, what is the matter? You look like you've lost your last friend."

Carrie pushed her bike into the garage. Kate's bike was not there. She walked slowly toward the house.

"Come on, old dear, tell me what is the matter."

Carrie sat down on the swing and told her mother about everything that had happened at the beach until she came to the confrontation on the raft. "I said some not very nice things to Kate," was all she said about that. "Here are the cookies Mrs. Riley gave to Kate. I wonder where she is now. Her bike's not in the garage."

71

"What?" Mother jumped up and ran into the house. Carrie was too tired to move. In a few minutes Mother returned.

"Snap out of it, Carrie," she ordered. "Go in and take a shower. That will make you feel better. Then make yourself a sandwich. I'm going to take a spin around the neighborhood. No, first you go check with Paul and Danny and see if they know where Kate is. Hurry!"

Carrie actually did hurry next door, but the boys hadn't seen Kate since they left the beach. Mother was backing the car out of the garage when Carrie returned. Mother's alarm was catching. By the time Carrie had showered and put on her thinnest shorts and briefest halter, the little stone in her stomach had grown to a basketball. She drank a big glass of orange juice and ate a few crackers. Then she opened the box of cookies and ate one of them.

Mother returned and went to the phone. "I don't know if we should be worried or not, Rob," Mother said. Then the door closed and Carrie heard no more until it opened again. "I'll call you if she comes back. I'll call you in an hour in any event." The receiver clicked, and then Mother was dialing again.

"May I speak to your mother?" Pause. "Hello. Joan Clark here. I just wanted to be sure that Alice is all right." Pause. Mother laughed. "I'm so sorry it happened, but I'm glad Alice survived so well. Thanks too for the cookies you sent to Kate. I know, but Carrie brought them home. No, I'm afraid that Kate is mad at all mothers at this point in her life." Pause. "The truth is, she's gone." Pause. "Yes, I've driven all around town and I can't find her. I was visiting a neighbor when she came home. I know she was here because her bathing suit is on the line and there are crumbs on the counter. That would indicate that she'd made a sandwich. . . . No note or anything, so I expect she's just gone for a few hours to give us all a chance to cool off. . . . Thank you."

"Where do you think Kate is?" Carrie asked her mother.

"I don't know."

An hour later Mother took another ride around town and out onto the parkway. No Kate. When she came back she phoned Daddy again.

Daddy came home early. In the meantime, Carrie's thoughts were turning round and round in her mind like sheets in the dryer. *"Mean, nasty, despicable, horrible. Too bad about your mother. Your mother left you. Mean, nasty . . ." Why did I say those words? Why did Kate run away? Did she run away? Maybe she is just hiding. . . . "Mean, nasty, despicable, horrible. . . ."*

Daddy and Mother went into a closed conference. Then they invited Carrie to come and tell them once again exactly what had happened at the beach. She told them, ending with, "And I said some not very nice things to Kate on the raft."

"Exactly what did you say?" asked Daddy.

Carrie hung her head. "Can't remember."

"Exactly what did you say?"

"I can't remember."

"Oh, yes, you can. Now. For the last time. Exactly what did you say to Kate?"

"I said she was mean, nasty, despicable and horrible." Carrie began to cry. "I said, 'Too bad about your mother.'"

Her own mother gasped.

"What else?" asked Daddy.

"I said, 'Your mother left you.'"

"And you had the nerve to call Kate mean, nasty, despicable and horrible. I'd say that you were the mean, nasty, despicable and horrible child." Daddy was not just angry; he was furious.

"But she tried to drown Alice. And she kicked the cookies Alice's mother gave to her."

"Go to your room and stay there," Daddy ordered.

As she was walking away, she heard Mother say, "You'd better go call Richard and Janet now. See if they want us to call the state troopers."

9

Carrie lay down on her bed and cried and cried. Then she slept and slept. It was dark when she awoke, and she lay on her bed, feeling confused. Then it all came back to her like Alice's lake sucking her down to the bottom.

She went to the door of her room. There were lights on in the living room downstairs.

"Daddy," she called. "I'm sorry, Daddy. May I come down?"

"He's not here now, Carrie," Mother answered. "But yes, you may come down."

Carrie went to the bathroom and splashed cold water on her face and combed her hair. Then she tiptoed down the stairs. Mother was sitting alone on the porch. For the first time, Carrie noticed that it was not night-dark so much as storm-dark. Thunder rumbled in the distance. She sat down close to her mother.

"Have a good sleep?" Mother asked, hugging her.

"Bet you're hungry. I left your dinner in the refrigerator."

"What about Kate?" Carrie whispered.

"There's been no word. Daddy is out with the car looking for her. So are the troopers. Uncle Richard and Aunt Janet are on their way."

"I shouldn't have said those things to Kate. I'm sorry."

"No, you shouldn't have, but there's nothing to be done about it. You were frightened. I'm glad you could help Alice."

"But I couldn't. I couldn't get her head above the water. All I could do was shout for help."

"That's all that was required of you, Carrie. Let's get you something to eat."

Mother put the food out on the table and poured herself a glass of iced tea.

"I think we'd better pray," she said, and she did. She asked God to take care of Kate and she asked for guidance in helping her.

Carrie prayed silently, asking God to forgive her for being so nasty.

When Carrie finished dinner, they went back to the porch and watched the storm come closer and closer. The rumbles and flashes matched Carrie's mood. Finally there was a flash that lit up the sky like day and a mighty crash of thunder. The sky opened up and rain poured down. While Carrie was closing the upstairs windows, she saw a car pull into the drive. A man and a woman got out and ran up on the porch.

"Any news?" the woman was calling. It was Aunt Janet.

Carrie ran down and stood beside her mother.

"None," said Mother quietly. "I'm so sorry, Janet. Richard."

"Rob's report was sketchy, so why don't you just tell us what happened," Uncle Richard suggested as they all sat down on the porch. "Where is Rob?"

"He's looking for her. So are the troopers. She's apparently on her bike."

"In this downpour?" Aunt Janet sounded shocked.

"Maybe she's found shelter someplace." Mother went on to tell Kate's parents about the events of the morning. When she reached the part about Kate leaving Alice in the deep water, Aunt Janet interrupted.

"How unlike Kate. She's always been so sensible and mature."

"Nevertheless, she's a child, and she has been withdrawn and obviously miserable with us." Mother continued to tell about events at the lake. When she got to the part about Carrie swimming out to the raft, she said, "Carrie was terribly upset and gave Kate a real tongue-lashing."

"I can understand why Carrie would be angry," said Uncle Richard.

"But why didn't you save your friend yourself?" asked Aunt Janet.

"Carrie does not swim as well as Kate. She tried to

hold Alice up and she called for help. That was all that was required of her." Mother was sounding very polite and icy as she went on to tell about Kate burying the cookies and riding off on the bike. "I'm sorry I wasn't home when she got here. Unfortunately, I was visiting a neighbor."

"I don't understand what the cookies have to do with all of this," Uncle Richard said.

"I don't either, really," said Mother. "Alice brought the cookies to Kate. They were a gift from her mother to thank Kate for helping Alice to learn to swim."

"So why didn't Kate just accept the cookies?" asked Aunt Janet.

"I think that Kate resents Alice's mother," said Mother slowly. "Several weeks ago she said that Mrs. Riley was disgusting."

"Would you let Carrie associate with a child whose mother was disgusting?" asked Aunt Janet.

"Alice is a lovely child and has been Carrie's best friend for many years. Her father and I teach together. Her mother is a particularly wholesome, pleasant woman whom I admire wholeheartedly."

"So why does she disgust Kate?" asked Uncle Richard.

"Mrs. Riley is the mother of five children. Kate tells us that it is sinful to have more than two children in this day and age. Mrs. Riley is also an enthusiastic homemaker. She bakes bread and health cookies and concentrates her energies on her home. Kate feels that she is wasting her talents." Mother stopped and took a deep breath. "Kate is intensely loyal to you, Janet. . . ."

"But she is jealous of Alice, whose mother is all the things I am not." Aunt Janet began to cry quietly. "I thought Kate was so independent. I thought she understood my need to be my own person. I guess I have not really understood *her* needs. But I do love her. I wonder if she knows that?"

"I think she does. Kate is very proud of you, Janet. Rob thinks she is probably biking to New York to be with you."

"One hundred and fifty miles alone on a bicycle!" exclaimed Uncle Richard.

"She wasn't thinking rationally when she set out." Mother sighed.

They sat in silence for a long time, listening to the distant rolls of thunder and the gentle drip of rain on the porch roof. Carrie thought about Aunt Janet and Uncle Richard. When she'd seen them arrive together, she had hoped that they might be making up and deciding not to get a divorce. But now they were sitting in chairs as far apart as they could be and still be on the same porch. Mother and Daddy always reached out for one another when they were upset or unhappy. Kate's parents were not reaching out.

The clock inside struck eleven at the same time that the telephone rang. Mother rushed to answer it. Kate's parents followed her.

"Rob checking in to see if there was any news,"

Mother explained when she put down the receiver.

"Where is Rob now?" asked Uncle Richard.

"About fifty miles down on Route 22. He's heading back this way. I think I'll lay out the makings for sandwiches and some coffee," Mother said and went to the kitchen. Carrie followed her.

In a little while they were all sitting around the kitchen table, but no one was eating. Aunt Janet was clicking her fingernails on the table and sipping coffee. Uncle Richard made himself a sandwich, but the first bite seemed to choke him. Suddenly he jumped up and announced that he was going off to search for Kate himself.

After a few gentle prods from Mother, Carrie went to bed. When Mother came up to say good-night, she promised that she would wake Carrie as soon as there was any news.

Carrie could not sleep. She lay in the dark and pictured Kate lying under a dripping tree on wet grass, trying to sleep. Was she really trying to get to New York or had she, perhaps, gone in the opposite direction, trying to get away from them all? Maybe she wasn't on her bike at all, but had hidden it someplace so they would all think she was on the road. Maybe she was really in the woods.

Carrie tried to plan what she would do if she were going to run away. She'd take a sleeping bag and pajamas, and underwear, and jeans in case it got cold, and a jacket or a sweat shirt, and several polo shirts and books. Carrie couldn't go anyplace without a supply of books. And food: bread, peanut butter, lemonade mix, fruit. She pictured all those things strapped to her bike, in the basket or hanging from the handlebars, and began to laugh. It was the first funny thought she had had all day.

The ringing of the phone broke the silence of the night. Carrie jumped out of bed and tiptoed down the stairs.

"Thank God," she heard Mother cry. "Is she really fine? Oh, thank you, officer. My husband is looking on Route 22, and so is her father. Thank you." Mother hung up. "Come on down, Carrie," she called. "Oh, Janet, they found her huddled under the roof of an abandoned gas station just off the Taconic Parkway, forty miles down the road. Can you imagine? She'd ridden her bike forty miles. The trooper is bringing her home. Now if we could only reach Rob and Richard."

As if Daddy knew that Mother wanted him, he phoned. He had met Uncle Richard and the two of them were heading home.

Carrie and her mother and her aunt went back to the porch to wait. The rain had stopped and there was a cool breeze, so cool that Carrie cuddled close to her mother for warmth. Her head fell forward. Her eyes felt heavy. So what if she slept? The squad car with its flashing lights and siren would awaken her. Kate was safe and coming home. . . . She awoke with a jerk. The squad car was in the driveway.

Where were the flashing lights? The siren? The door slammed and Kate was walking toward the house. Carrie jumped up to run and greet her, but her mother pulled her back. Aunt Janet stepped forward.

"Hello, Kate," she said and held out her arms.

"Hello, Mom." Kate walked around her mother and up on the porch.

Two more cars pulled into the driveway.

"Kate," Uncle Richard called.

"Sorry, Aunt Joan," Kate said and walked into the house.

They could hear her footsteps on the stairs.

"Kate," Uncle Richard called again as he ran into the house. In a few minutes he was back. "She's tired, poor kid!" he said as he sat down and buried his head in his hands. "Did she say anything to you, officer?" he asked.

"Nothing." The trooper went to the squad car and lifted Kate's bike out of the trunk.

Carrie's father went with him, and she saw the two men shaking hands.

"Let's go to bed," Mother suggested. "Would you like to sleep in Carrie's bed?" she asked Aunt Janet.

Aunt Janet shook her head. "I'd like to be near her, but I think she'd rather not be near me. She just doesn't understand, does she?"

Carrie ran upstairs. Kate was already in bed with the sheet pulled over her head.

"I'm glad you're home," Carrie said.

"I have no home," Kate mumbled.

10

Sun was streaming into the room when Carrie awoke. She could hear voices downstairs and smell bacon frying. She looked at her clock. It was ten. Too late for swimming lessons. She looked over to the other bed. Kate was lying on her back, staring at the ceiling. Her face was streaked with dirt. She turned and saw Carrie looking at her.

"Hi," said Carrie softly.

Kate jumped out of bed, took clean clothes out of her still packed suitcase, and went to the bathroom. When she returned she looked all clean and fresh. Her hair was wrapped in a towel.

"Did you really ride forty miles?" Carrie asked.

"Guess I did." Kate grinned.

"I'm sorry about the mean things I said out on the raft yesterday. I guess I was just scared for Alice, but Alice isn't mad. In fact, I think she's all over being frightened of the water."

"I know." That was all Kate said, but somehow Carrie knew that she was forgiven.

No one said much during breakfast, but everyone was so hungry and the waffles and eggs and bacon were so good that it didn't matter. After breakfast, Kate and Uncle Richard and Aunt Janet all got into Uncle Richard's car and drove off.

"Where are they going?" Carrie asked, afraid that they were going back to New Jersey without Kate's bike or any of her things.

"They're going to look at the boarding school in Lenox," Daddy explained. "Richard called for an appointment today. Then I suppose they'll discuss future plans."

"Couldn't they just go back to New Jersey and live together like they used to?" Carrie asked. "That would be the simplest plan, and I'll bet that is what Kate would like best."

"I'm sure that's what Kate would like best, but it isn't what she's going to get. Richard is going to Tulsa. Janet is staying in New York. Their house is being sold. The divorce is going forward." Daddy sounded cross.

"And we have to talk about the future, too," Mother said softly.

Just for a moment Carrie had a wild fear. Suppose her folks were also getting a divorce. Then she looked at them, and they were standing close together and holding hands. They weren't about to move away from one another. Carrie went and stood beside them, and they gathered together in a three-way hug. It was a nice warm hug.

"We have to decide if we want to ask Kate to join our family on a permanent basis," said Mother.

"Kate isn't an easy person to live with," said Daddy. "But we know that she is hurting, and we could expect her to be more pleasant once she got adjusted."

"She was very nice during that week after she wrote to Uncle Richard," said Carrie.

"That's true. She'll never be a chatterbox like one girl I know." He gave Carrie a little slap. "And that chatterbox is used to being an only child. In fact, we've been a pretty close threesome for a number of years now. So the question is, do we want to share our home permanently with another child?"

"I had just been planning for the summer," Carrie said. "I hadn't planned for ever and ever and ever."

"Neither had we," said Mother. "That's why we must consider this very carefully. Kate has had too much interruption in her life already. If we ask her to stay, our invitation will be permanent and irrevocable. We will keep her with us until she is grown, no matter what."

"But . . ." Carrie couldn't go on. She couldn't imagine life with Kate for ever and ever. She liked being an only child. She had thought she wanted a sister, but Kate was too different from the sister she had imagined. She had made changes in Carrie's life already, and they weren't changes Carrie liked. But . . . Where would Kate go? To boarding school? Kate didn't want to go to boarding school. She didn't want to live with them either. "Kate wouldn't have run away if she had wanted to live with us," Carrie said.

"That's true," said Daddy, "but she doesn't have many alternatives, does she?"

"She doesn't like me."

"She doesn't like any of us very much right now," Mother said.

"Maybe she'd learn to like us if she knew she was stuck with us."

"You make us sound like monsters." Daddy laughed. "We know that we are really very nice people, and we have been happy together. Maybe we should share our happiness."

When Daddy put it that way, what could Carrie say? "OK. Let's invite her to stay."

"She may not accept our invitation," Mother said, "but if she does, we'll move everything in the sewing room to the basement and repaint that room a color Kate chooses. Uncle Richard can have her furniture shipped here, and that will make her feel more at home. It will also give you girls a chance to be apart. We'll see to it that you are in different classes in school. Maybe we'll paint your room, too. And get you new bedspreads and curtains."

"Drapes?" asked Carrie. "I could push the beds into

the corner so they'd look like a couch. My room could be my study. I could put the desk beside the dresser and . . ."

"She's off," said Daddy. "Planning, planning, planning." He picked up a stack of plates and headed for the kitchen.

Those best laid schemes went a-gley too. When Kate and her parents returned late in the afternoon, they had made all of their own plans. Daddy said they would welcome Kate as a permanent member of their family. Mother said she could have her own room with her own furniture. Carrie said they'd be in different classes in school. Kate just shook her head.

Uncle Richard did the talking. They would all three leave in the morning. They would take Aunt Janet back to the city, and she would see about a bigger apartment. He and Kate would go to New Jersey to begin packing their things. Aunt Janet would come and help them over the weekend. Then he and Kate would go to the shore for a few days—before he went to Tulsa and she went to New York to stay with Aunt Janet until her school started in September. While Uncle Richard was talking, Aunt Janet was stroking Kate's hair.

One of Carrie's plans finally did work out. That night when they went to bed, Kate and Carrie talked. Kate talked about her new school, the Olympic-sized

swimming pool, the huge playing fields. Many of the students at that school had divorced parents.

"I'm sorry you decided not to live with us," Carrie said, and found that she meant it. "I had hoped we could be sisters."

"Sisters have the same parents. Your parents are quite different from mine." Kate stopped for a minute. Then she went on in a rush. "But mine both love me very much. I know that for absolutely sure. I'm going to spend Christmas and part of next summer with Daddy in Tulsa. Did you know that the dirt in Oklahoma is red? I'll spend other vacations with my mother. She really does want me, you know. She says we'll go to the theater and to art shows. I'd rather go to a Mets game, but I'll tell her that later. I think it will be a rather nice life."

"When will I see you?" Carrie asked.

"Maybe I'll come for short vacations and weekends," Kate said. "We can't be sisters, but we are cousins after all." She reached across the space between the beds, and patted Carrie's arm.

Carrie wanted to leap into her bed and kiss her, but she didn't. Kate wouldn't have liked that.